and friends

★ ★ ★

The Talent Show

The Talent Show

HarperCollins *Children's Books*

MEET
HELLO KITTY
and friends

Mimmy

Hello Kitty

Tammy

Mama

Papa

Grandpa

Grandma

Fifi

Dear Daniel

With special thanks to
Linda Chapman and Michelle Misra

First published in Great Britain by HarperCollins *Children's Books* in 2013

www.harpercollins.co.uk
1 3 5 7 9 10 8 6 4 2
ISBN: 978-0-00-751576-9

Printed and bound in England by Clays Ltd, St Ives plc.

MIX
Paper from
responsible sources
FSC C007454

FSC™ is a non-profit international organisation established to promote
the responsible management of the world's forests. Products carrying the
FSC label are independently certified to assure consumers that they come
from forests that are managed to meet the social, economic and
ecological needs of present and future generations,
and other controlled sources.

Find out more about HarperCollins and the environment at
www.harpercollins.co.uk/green

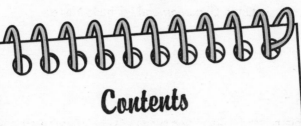

Contents

1. Dressing Up.....................9

2. Decisions, Decisions.............22

3. Dear Daniel's Idea.............36

4. Makeover Fun.................56

5. Talent on Show.............79

Dressing Up

Brrrring! Hello Kitty rang the doorbell.
She waited excitedly as she heard the sound
of running footsteps and then the door was
thrown open. Her friends Fifi, Tammy and Dear
Daniel, stood inside. They were all members

of the Friendship Club, which they had started together after they all met at school. They held fun meetings, went on trips out together and made up rules about friendship.

That Saturday they were having a *special* Friendship Club meeting at Fifi's – they had

decided to hold a toy fashion show! Hello Kitty had her fluffy white bear with her. She could see that all her friends had toys too – Fifi had a tiger, Tammy had a rabbit and Dear Daniel had a zebra. Hello Kitty couldn't wait to get started!

They all said hello and hurried upstairs. Fifi had made a catwalk for the toys in her bedroom. She had made it out of shoeboxes glued

together with material stuck on top. It looked

really **super!** All the toys had come from

a special shop where you could buy different

clothes to dress your toy in. The four friends put

the outfits they had brought on to Fifi's bed and

then they each selected

something for their toy

to wear. Dear Daniel

wanted Stripy his

zebra to wear sporty clothes. But would it be a football kit or a karate kit or a skateboard kit? He decided on the football kit.

Tammy put Floppy, her toy rabbit, into a denim skirt and white T-shirt while Fifi dressed Tasha the tiger in a purple *sparkly* ice skating outfit with matching ice skates. Hello Kitty took much longer to decide on what her toy bear, Snowflake,

would be wearing. It was so much fun trying

out different tops with different skirts, adding

scarves and belts and hairbands until the outfit

looked perfect. **Almost** like being a real

fashion designer!

While they were waiting for Hello Kitty,

Tammy picked up Floppy

and Stripy and started

pretending to make

them talk in silly

voices. She made

Stripy ask Floppy for a

dance and then made

Floppy act as if she was

really shy! Fifi, Hello Kitty and Dear Daniel giggled loudly. So Tammy put on the same voice as their class teacher Miss Davey had, when she got cross and told them to settle

down. She sounded so much like Miss Davey that they all *giggled* even more.

But now Hello Kitty was finally ready! Snowflake was wearing a short ruffled red skirt with a white T-shirt, and a red and black striped waistcoat. She had a matching red and black hairband, with a sparkly bow and a little red

handbag. She looked **super-stylish!**

Tammy remarked how nice Snowflake looked. She wished Floppy looked as good but

she could never work out what clothes went together. Hello Kitty smiled and offered to help her. She loved helping her friends! She

swapped Floppy's plain white

T-shirt for a strappy pale

blue top with a heart on it,

and then chose a navy and

pink scarf that she

twisted around Floppy's neck.

She added a navy belt

and shoes and then

finished the look off

with a blue hair bow.

She nodded at

Tammy and

wondered what

she thought now.

It turned out that Tammy loved Floppy's new look! Hello Kitty was so **clever!** Fifi and Dear Daniel agreed. Hello Kitty felt a little bit embarrassed but very pleased. She blushed bright pink.

Tammy looked down
at her own jeans and
plain blue T-shirt and
sighed – she wished
Hello Kitty could style
HER!

And then one of her
super, special Hello Kitty ideas came into
Hello Kitty's head. Maybe she could!

But before she could say anything, Fifi's
mum came into the bedroom. She had just
read something very exciting in the new school
newsletter… Their school was going to be
holding a talent show next weekend to raise

SCHOOL TALENT SHOW

Open for entries NOW!

What's your talent?

NEXT WEEKEND!

money for some play equipment! Any pupil at

the school could enter and the winner would

get a silver cup. Did they want to go in for it,

she asked?

The four friends jumped up and down

in excitement. They certainly did! But

WHAT could each of them do?

2

Decisions, Decisions...

The Friendship Club sat down together on the floor. The toys' fashion show could wait for the moment. Right now they needed to decide what they could all do in the school talent show. Dear Daniel said he would play his guitar – he

could play one of the songs he had written. The others thought that was a great idea!

Fifi wished she could ice-skate in the show. She was really good at skating but there wasn't an ice rink at school so she would have to choose something else. **Hmmm...** Hello Kitty suggested that Fifi do some gymnastics. Fifi loved that idea!

She could wear a sparkly leotard and do a routine to music.

But what about Hello Kitty and Tammy?

Hello Kitty thought about the things she liked doing. She **l♥ved** fashion and baking but neither of those things would be right for a talent show act.

Tammy had an idea – what if she did singing or dancing? Hello Kitty nodded thoughtfully. She did love both of those things. Maybe she could perform a song by her favourite band – the

Fizzy Pops!
She would add
some dance
moves in too!
Would Tammy
like to join in with her?

But Tammy didn't like

singing in front of an audience unless she was

part of a bigger group of people. She said she

would do something else — but she couldn't

think what...

Everyone thought hard. What **could**

Tammy do? She liked reading, making up stories

and playing practical jokes. But none of those

things could be a talent show act. Dear Daniel

suggested she joined in playing a song with him

but Tammy only played the recorder, and she

didn't think that would sound right with Dear

Daniel's guitar.

So Fifi asked Tammy to do a gymnastics

routine with her. Tammy looked uncertain. She

wasn't very good at gymnastics – not like Fifi.
Fifi encouraged her and said she was sure she
would be fine, so Tammy tried a cartwheel in
the bedroom but it went wrong and she fell in
a heap. Gymnastics SO wasn't her talent. What
COULD she do?

They all agreed to keep thinking about it but they would have to think fast because there was only a week to practise their acts! Hello Kitty *gasped*. She'd just had a brilliant idea! Why didn't they all come to her house for a sleepover on Friday to do a final practice? It was the night before the contest. And she remembered what she'd been going to say earlier – she could also do a makeover on Tammy then, if Tammy wanted! Tammy loved the thought of it and Fifi and Dear Daniel were keen to come along and practice for the talent show. It would be a really fun night! Hello Kitty beamed – she would ask her mama if it was OK on the way home. But now, what about the fashion show? It was time for their toys to show off their outfits and dance down the catwalk!

Playing at fashion shows was great fun and

afterwards they ate home-made

pizza and ice cream before

their parents came to

pick them up. Hello

Kitty's twin sister Mimmy

was in the car with Mama.

Hello Kitty told them all about

the school talent show. Mama said it sounded

very **exciting** and

Mimmy wanted to enter

too – she said she

would play her flute

with her friend, Alice.

As soon as they got home Mimmy went to phone Alice and Hello Kitty ran upstairs to listen to some songs by the Fizzy Pops. She had to choose which one she wanted to sing but it was so hard because she loved them all! In the end she had narrowed it down to three songs…

Here Comes the Moonlight

Missing You

Sunshine Girl

She practised them all but couldn't decide which one to pick. In the end she thought she would ask her friends' advice the next day at school instead of choosing by herself.

Mama called up the stairs – it was bedtime for the twins! Hello Kitty got into her pyjamas and **snuggled** down in bed with one of her favourite magazines. It had an article about

doing makeovers. Hello Kitty read it eagerly.

There was useful advice about what colour

clothes went with different hair and skin tones,

and some good make-up and hair tips. And then

there were some suggestions for different looks,

but Hello Kitty had **lots** of ideas of her own!

She wanted to do a party look and a daytime

look for Tammy. She read the final paragraph...

Makeovers are great fun but don't try to change your friends too much! Everyone is different so remember not to try to make them look just like you or just like a fashion model in a magazine – a makeover should help someone find their OWN style. You are there to help their inner beauty shine through!

Fashion Forward Magazine **33**

Hello Kitty closed the magazine thoughtfully. The article was very true. She didn't want to change Tammy, just help her look the best she could.

Excitement *fizzed* up inside her as she started planning possible outfits in her head. A makeover AND a talent show next weekend – how exciting was that!

Dear Daniel's Idea

On Monday, the Friendship Club got together

at break time to talk about the talent show.

Everyone in their class wanted to enter too!

Hello Kitty had got her three songs ready.

Her friends listened to her as she sang them all,

and then voted on the song they

thought sounded best. They

chose *Sunshine Girl*. Hello

Kitty had also thought up a

really COOl dance routine

that went with it really well.

She showed them how it went and

Tammy made a few suggestions for some extra

dance moves.

Then they all listened to Dear Daniel on his

guitar and Fifi performed her

gymnastics routine. They

clapped as she finished

with a back flip.

Tammy pretended to be a judge and put on a voice like their head teacher, Mrs Brown, and told Fifi she was *brilliant* and had scored ten out of ten! They all giggled. Suddenly Hello Kitty realised that they still hadn't helped Tammy think of something to do. That had to be their next task!

But still no one could think of **anything.**

Tammy said she thought it might be easier if she

didn't enter – she was happy to just cheer them

all on.

But the rest of The Friendship Club didn't

want Tammy to be left out. She HAD to enter!

Dear Daniel announced that he **might** have an idea. He wasn't going to tell them now but if they were allowed to come round to his house after school he would hold a Friendship Club meeting and tell them then.

Just then, the bell rang and they had to go back into class. Hello Kitty ran inside with the others, her mind racing. What was Dear Daniel's idea for Tammy's act going to be?

Dear Daniel lived in a little house with a white fence around the front garden and a green front door. His dad let the girls in and they went through to the big sunroom at the back of the house, where Dear Daniel was

waiting for them. He had a big box on the table

in front of him covered up with a purple cloth.

As they came in he whisked it off. Ta da!

Hello Kitty stared. On the table was a box of

Magic Tricks...

Maybe Tammy could be a magician!

Tammy giggled. She liked the thought of it,

but she had no idea if she was any

good at magic tricks. Dear

Daniel explained he would

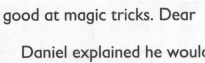

magic tricks

help her – his dad had taught him how to do magic tricks the last time they had been travelling abroad together. While he started showing Tammy what to do, Fifi and Hello Kitty practised their own acts. They could hear Tammy *laughing.* Hello Kitty didn't want to put her off by saying anything, but every time she looked round, Tammy seemed to be getting a trick wrong!

After a while, Dear Daniel's dad brought in a tray piled high with biscuits, flapjacks, glasses

and a big jug of blackcurrant squash. They all
had a snack and a drink and then Dear Daniel
said he thought Tammy was ready to show
them some tricks.

Tammy didn't look quite as sure, but she
went and dressed up in the magician's cape
and hat and then came back out. She had also
stuck a very large fake moustache on her face.
She twirled it round and put
on a funny voice – telling
them she was Mervyn the
Magnificent Magician!

The others all giggled.
She sounded very funny.

Tammy threw her arms wide and told

them to prepare to be AMAZED,

ASTOUNDED and ASTONISHED.

   She looked really confident as she did

a twirl, *swirling* out her cape, and then she

took out a pack of cards. She asked Hello Kitty

to choose one but not show it to her. It was

the Queen of Hearts. Tammy took out another

pack of cards and shuffled it and pulled out a

card from the middle. She showed it to them.

Had she chosen the same

card as Hello Kitty?

Hello Kitty looked

at the ace of spades

in Tammy's hand. It

wasn't the same card

at all! **Oh dear**.

She showed Tammy the

card in her hand.

Tammy looked a bit embarrassed

and tried again but this time she

47

pulled out the two of diamonds. Her card trick really wasn't working, so she *quickly* moved on to the next trick. She announced she was going to perform a MAGICAL, MIRACULOUS and MARVELLOUS trick – she was going to pull a toy rabbit from her empty hat!

She took her hat off
and showed them it
was empty inside.
Only… it wasn't.
Fifi put up her hand
and whispered to
Tammy that she could see
a long fluffy white ear sticking out of the hat's
purple lining. **Whoops!** Tammy giggled and

quickly stuffed the ear back
inside. Now that trick
had gone wrong too!
Maybe she should try
another one instead!

But trick after trick went wrong. Tammy

started to giggle more and more with every

mistake. The others started to laugh too – they

couldn't help it. It was so funny and Tammy

didn't mind that they were all laughing! In

fact, she started to mess around even more

and made mistakes on purpose. In the end

she pulled off her cape and hat. It had been a

great idea of Dear Daniel's but she didn't

think she had better be a magician in the talent

show. Not unless she wanted to win a prize for

being the worst act on the stage!

So what WAS she going to do?

Tammy said she had made up her mind. She

really wasn't going to go in the

show. The others started

to argue with her but

she shook her head.

She really, really didn't

mind. She told them

she was very happy just helping them and not entering herself! After all, not everyone in the world had a talent that was right for a talent show, and that was **OK.**

She would help them get ready and then watch from the audience.

Fifi and Dear Daniel still wanted to persuade

her to enter but Hello Kitty remembered what

she had read the night before about how you

shouldn't try and make a friend be just like you.

If Tammy was **happy** not entering then that

should be fine with her friends!

She gave Tammy a hug and said that it would

be **l♥vely** to have her watch and help

them even if she wasn't entering. Fifi and Dear

Daniel hugged her too. Hello Kitty checked that

even if Tammy didn't go in the show she would

still come to the sleepover on Friday night.

Wouldn't she? Tammy **grinned.** Just try

and stop her!

Makeover Fun

Hello Kitty *skipped* around her bedroom getting everything ready for the sleepover. It was after school on Friday and very soon the rest of the Friendship Club would be arriving. All week, she and Fifi and Dear Daniel had been

practising their acts. Tammy had been a great
help, watching them and giving them tips. Hello
Kitty was **really** looking forward to doing the
makeover on Tammy – it would be one way of
saying thank you to her for being so supportive.
Tammy really was a BRILLIANT friend!

Hello Kitty had placed some duvets out on her bedroom floor. They were all going to have sleeping bags on top of the duvets and sleep there. Her own sleeping bag, which was pink with purple **polka dots** all over it, was already carefully laid out. Next to it was a white sleeping bag covered with red hearts. That was Mimmy's – Hello Kitty's twin sister. She was joining in the sleepover. She wasn't a regular member of The Friendship Club because she played the flute and was too busy with band practice but she liked to

HELLO KITTY *and friends*

join in with the things they did when she could.

Hello Kitty's bed had different accessories

laid out on it. There were…

Scarves

Belts

Hair bows

Fabric pens

A sewing kit

Tammy was going to bring some old clothes with her that her mum didn't mind being customised and changed.

Hello Kitty quickly tidied the dressing table. She collected lip glosses and she put them all out in a neat row along with…

Sparkly eye shadow

Hair brushes

Glitter spray

Perfume

There! She was ready for her friends to arrive. Mimmy came running into the bedroom with a bag in her hands.

On her way back from band

practice she had asked Papa

to stop at the shops and

she had bought some

sweets for a midnight feast.

Perfect!

The twins split the sweets

into five little bowls and then there

was a knock on the front door. Their guests

had arrived. The sleepover was about to begin!

Soon everyone had put out their sleeping

bags and unpacked their pyjamas and

toothbrushes. Tammy gave Hello Kitty the

bag of clothes she had brought for them to

customise. Fifi had also brought some old

clothes that her mum had said Hello Kitty could

use for the makeover if she wanted. While

Dear Daniel, Fifi and Mimmy went into Mimmy's

bedroom to practise for the talent show, Hello

Kitty and Tammy put all the makeover clothes

out on the bed.

Tammy shook her head and breathed that

it looked like a jumble sale! She had **no**

idea how Hello Kitty would be

able to make her look nice with

these old clothes. But Hello Kitty's mind was already filling with ideas. **Hmmm.** There were several skirts; T-shirts; leggings; some too-small summer dresses; old jeans with a rip in them and a sparkly dress of Fifi's. She started to pull clothes together,

trying out looks and then changing her mind. If she'd been choosing for herself she would definitely have gone for

65

one of the ruffled skirts for the daytime look

and paired it with some *cool* accessories,

but she wasn't choosing an outfit for herself.

She was choosing one for Tammy and she knew

Tammy liked to wear jeans and T-shirts.

Finally, Hello Kitty made up her mind. She cut

three squares out of some old pink and purple

patterned blouses and then handed them to

Tammy with the sewing kit and the jeans. She

wanted Tammy to sew the **brightly**

coloured patches over the rips in the jeans. It

would stop them looking old and would make

them much more stylish. Tammy set to work.

Meanwhile, Hello Kitty pulled out

an old lilac summer dress.

If she shortened it, it

would make a great

daytime tunic to

go over the jeans.

To complete the look,

Tammy could wear a red

and white scarf wrapped twice around her neck.

Perfect!

Mama White peeped round the door to see

how they were getting on. She loved fashion

and wanted to see what the girls were up to!

Hello Kitty showed her what she wanted to

do with the tunic and Mama said she would

shorten it using her sewing machine. She took

the tunic out to start on it.

While Tammy sewed the patches on to the jeans, Hello Kitty began to think about the party look. This was so much **fun!**

At last, the clothes were all ready. Tammy dressed up in the jeans and tunic and they looked fantastic! Hello Kitty showed Tammy how to tie the scarf around her neck, and then started to do her hair and make-up. She backcombed Tammy's hair and fixed it in a high

ponytail, and then she added a little watermelon

lip gloss. Tammy was ready – her daytime look

was complete!

Tammy looked in the mirror and beamed in

delight. She **l♥ved** the fact she was still

wearing jeans but they looked so much more

stylish now that they had the purple

and pink patches sewn on them,

and they went really

well with the

lilac tunic

top. The

scarf around

her neck was the perfect finishing touch. Hello

Kitty called the others into her bedroom, and

they all rushed in and admired Tammy's new

look. She did a twirl and everyone clapped.

Mama announced that she would go and

start getting tea ready. She asked Mimmy, Fifi

and Dear Daniel to help her while Hello Kitty

helped Tammy into the party outfit.

Tammy changed out of the

jeans. For her party outfit,

Hello Kitty had turned

Fifi's silver **sparkly**

dress into a skirt, and

added a red chiffon scarf

as a belt. Because the skirt was so sparkly, Hello Kitty matched it with a simple white top, red and silver bangles and a small red shoulder bag. *Perfect* for a party! In fact, it would have been perfect for the talent show... Hello Kitty felt a tiny flash of disappointment that Tammy wasn't going to be entering.

74

But it was OK as long as Tammy was happy, she thought.

Hello Kitty showed Tammy how to apply silver eye shadow with a brush and then finished off the look by putting Tammy's hair up into a messy bun. She twisted Tammy's hair up and used hair grips to fix it into place. As she worked, Tammy picked up the hairbrush and comb and started to pretend that they were talking to

each other. She made the comb sound like their

class teacher, Miss Davey, and the hairbrush

sound like her twin brother, Timmy. Miss Davey

was **chasing** Timmy around, telling him

off for having untidy, sticking-up hair. Then

she picked up the eye

shadow brush and started

pretending that was Hello

Kitty trying to give Timmy a makeover! Hello

Kitty started giggling. Tammy was very

good at making her voice sound like other

people's. She should be on stage!

Hello Kitty suddenly gave a squeal. That was it! **Of course!** Why hadn't she thought about it before? Tammy COULD go in the talent show after all!

Talent on Show

Tammy **jumped** when Hello Kitty

squealed. Hello Kitty quickly explained her idea.

Why didn't Tammy perform imitations of people

at the talent show? She could imitate their

teacher Miss Davey and their head teacher

Mrs Brown – and maybe some of the other pupils like her brother Timmy.

Tammy stared at Hello Kitty. Would people *really* think her silly voices and imitations were funny?

Absolutely! Hello Kitty declared she was SURE they would. Tammy would be so good on stage – and her imitations always made people laugh. Tammy's eyes *sparkled*. This was the perfect act for her! She wanted to tell the others straightaway!

They raced downstairs. As soon as everyone heard about Hello Kitty's idea they all agreed it was great and that Tammy was going to look **fantastic** on stage in her new party outfit. Tammy was so excited. She was going to be in the talent show after all! But would they help her work out her act and what she was going to say?

They all grinned. DEFINITELY!

The rest of the sleepover *flew* by with them all helping Tammy and then performing their own acts for each other. They rehearsed again when they woke up the next morning.

Almost before they knew it, it was Saturday evening and time for the contest. They went into school with their parents. There was a big banner over the school entrance which said:

★ TALENT SHOW! ★

The parents headed into the hall to sit down while everyone who had entered went to one of the classrooms to get ready. Their names had been written on a whiteboard in the order they would go on stage. Hello Kitty was on first and Tammy was on last, and the others were in the middle. In

the classrooms, everyone was practising. Miss

Davey was overseeing everything. People were

getting changed, putting on make-up,

tuning up musical instruments,

singing scales and warming

up for dance routines. On

one side of the classroom,

Timmy was juggling five balls.

Near to the door,

Alice and Mimmy were

playing their flutes

together. A boy from

one of the other classes

84

had a skateboard with him and one girl had her
dog! It looked like the show was going to be full
of talent!

The Friendship Club all sat together as they
waited. Dear Daniel had his guitar. Hello Kitty
and Fifi each had the music for their routines
with them. Fifi was dressed in a **sparkly**
green leotard with a matching hair ribbon.

Hello Kitty had chosen to wear a pink leotard with a tutu, and matching pink legwarmers for her dance and song. Tammy was dressed in her new party outfit. She looked great!

Dear Daniel asked her if she was glad she was entering. Tammy nodded, and replied that she couldn't wait to get on stage. She hoped people thought she was **funny!**

Suddenly, Miss Davey clapped her hands and called for silence. She asked them all to bring their

things and follow her – they would be sitting at
the side of the stage, waiting their turn.

They all followed her to the hall and sat
down. The judges – three of the other teachers
– were sitting at a table at the side of the stage.
The head teacher, Mrs Brown, welcomed the
audience and wished everyone taking part good
luck. Then she called the first contestant on to
the stage. It was Hello Kitty! It was time for
the show to begin!

Hello Kitty barely had a chance to feel nervous.
She walked on stage and struck her starting pose.
Miss Davey started her music and Hello Kitty
started to sing and dance. She loved it! It was so

much fun performing one of her favourite songs for everyone. She finished with a perfect spin and then curtsied as everyone clapped loudly.

She glanced at the judges. They were smiling too and writing down their marks. Hello Kitty ran off the stage to her seat and then it was Timmy's turn to show off his juggling skills.

Act followed act. Everyone was *SOOO* good! Dear Daniel's song sounded great. Fifi did some amazing cartwheels and back flips and ended in the splits. Mimmy and Alice

played the tune *Greensleeves* on their flutes.

But the other contestants were great too!

Timmy had juggled really well without dropping

anything. The girl and her dog

did a dance and the boy with

the skateboard showed off

some cool tricks. Hello Kitty

l♥ved every second of it.

She realised she didn't care if she won

or not; she was just glad to be taking part.

At last it was Tammy's turn. When Mrs

Brown called out Tammy's name,

she looked a bit nervous. Hello

Kitty squeezed her hand and

90

reassured her she would be brilliant. Fifi and

Dear Daniel wished her luck. Taking a deep

breath, Tammy *ran* on to the stage. She

waited as the audience gradually quietened

down, and then she began.

She started by pretending to be the head teacher. As soon as she began speaking in Mrs Brown's voice, she started moving like her too. She pretended to tell the audience off and everyone started chuckling. Her nervousness started to drop away. She turned round, pulled a black wig out of her pocket and put it on. Then she turned back to the audience, immediately changing her voice so she sounded just like Miss Davey. She was **amazing!** Hello

Kitty saw Miss Davey smiling and then Tammy pulled off the wig and put on a pair of glasses to look like their music teacher, and then just kept changing characters as she went on. By the end of her act the audience were all laughing and clapping. The judges were **smiling** too. Tammy got a huge round of applause – the biggest of the evening!

She ran back to the others, her cheeks pink with happiness. Hello Kitty squeezed her hand. It had been such a great act – she really hoped

Tammy would win!

The judges stood up and said how astonished they were at all of the talent on show. Every one of the contestants should be **very** proud of themselves and it had been very hard to choose between them, but in the end they had

their three winners. They announced the results

in reverse order.

3rd place – Hello Kitty's *Sunshine Girl*

2nd place – Chloe and her Dancing Dog

1st place – Tammy and her Irresistible

Imitations!

The audience whooped and cheered as

the prize winners all ran on stage. Hello Kitty

and Chloe got small silver shields on wooden

plaques. Hello Kitty was delighted with hers!

She thanked the judge and then

watched proudly as Tammy

came up to get the big

silver cup and a simply

TALENT SHOW!

2nd

ENORMOUS box of chocolates tied up with a big blue ribbon. Mrs Brown smiled and said that next time she was ill she would give Tammy a call and let her keep order in the school! Everyone laughed, Tammy **grinned**, and then had to pose as someone took her photograph for the local paper. With that, the competition was over. Dear Daniel and Fifi raced over to hug Tammy and Hello Kitty. What an amazing result! Only yesterday

Tammy hadn't even thought she was entering the show and now she had **won** it!

Tammy said it was all thanks to Hello Kitty and the others. She would never have thought of entering her imitations if Hello Kitty hadn't suggested it and everyone had been so supportive. She thought they should have a new Friendship Club rule.

Good friends help find your hidden talents.

They all high-fived each other. It was a perfect new rule for them! **Super!**

Tammy grinned. Now there was just one thing left for the Friendship Club to help with – eating her chocolates!

The end

Turn over the page for activities and fun things that you can do with your friends – just like Hello Kitty!

Talent on Show!

Hello Kitty had so much fun at the talent show, and now you and your friends can too! Follow the instructions to set up your very own so you can amaze each other with your skills...

You will need:

- Somewhere to hold your talent show
- Friends and family to enter – and to watch and vote!
- Equipment: a music system, chairs for an audience etc.
- Pens and paper for voting
- Costumes and props for the acts
- A prize for the winner!

Tricks and Talents

You and your friends will need to decide what you want to do! Juggling, singing or dancing? Playing an instrument or telling a joke?

But don't worry if you're not perfect at something – the important thing is that you have fun!

Once you have picked, get practising. And don't forget your costume!

It's Talent Time!

1. Decide where you will hold your show — you will need a stage area, and space for people to sit and watch.

2. Next, list who is performing and what they will do, and decide the order they will appear in.

3. Make a list of any equipment you need, like a music player if people will be dancing.

4. Host a dress rehearsal. Ask everyone to come dressed up as they would for the show. This should be just like the real thing, but without the audience.

5. On with the show! Have fun performing, and watching your friends!

And the winner is...

To pick a winner, have everyone write the name of their favourite act on a piece of paper and hand them in. Count them up at the end, and the person with the most votes wins!

The winner will need a prize too – nothing too big! They could have sweets, or a special certificate you decorate yourself.

So no one misses out, you could give out other prizes too! Why not try out some of these:

- *The funniest act*
- *Practised the most*
- *The silliest act*

Magical Mystery!

Some magic can be your eyes playing tricks on you. In this trick, you can put a bird in a cage by twirling your fingers!

ALWAYS ASK A GROWN-UP FOR HELP BEFORE USING SCISSORS!

You will need:

A round piece of cardboard, about 6cm across

Scissors

A Pen

String

Copy the template below on to your piece of cardboard. (There are pictures on both sides).

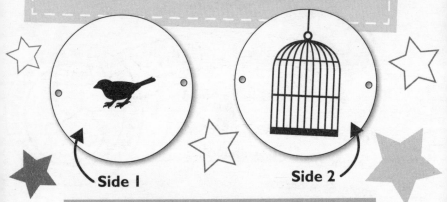

Side 1   Side 2

Tie a piece of string through the hole on each side as shown, and twirl the string in your fingers quickly, so the card spins.

Ta da!

Your eyes will be tricked into seeing the bird inside the cage.

Turn the page for a sneak peek at

and friends'

VERY SPECIAL

next adventure...

The Christmas Present
·A HELLO KITTY CHRISTMAS SPECIAL·

Hello Kitty crossed her arms and sat up as straight as she could as Miss Davey, her teacher, looked around the class. Hello Kitty was wishing hard that Miss Davey would call on her. Every day since the first of December, Miss Davey had chosen one person to go up to the front and open the next door of the advent calendar.

Miss Davey's eyes settled on Hello Kitty and she smiled. Today would be Hello Kitty's turn! Hello Kitty jumped to her feet and hurried to Miss Davey's desk. She found the little door marked with the number '5' and opened it carefully. What would the picture be?

It was a beautiful Christmas tree decorated with coloured balls and tinsel. Mrs Davey asked Hello Kitty to carry the calendar round and show it to the whole class. She hoped that the class would make sure the school's very own Christmas tree looked just as beautiful by the end of the day.

They all nodded excitedly. Their class had been picked to decorate the school Christmas tree! It was going to be delivered at lunchtime and they were going to get out the decorations and make it look lovely and festive. Hello Kitty felt just super even thinking about it! She loved Christmas! She loved everything about it, especially…

Putting up decorations

Singing carols

Hanging up her stocking

And PRESENTS of course!

Find out what happens next in...

Coming soon:

· A HELLO KITTY CHRISTMAS SPECIAL ·

TWO SPECIAL CHRISTMAS STORIES

HELLO KITTY
and friends

The Christmas Present

HELLO KITTY
The Friendship Club

HELLO KITTY
and friends
The School Trip

HELLO KITTY
and friends
The Summer Fair

HELLO KITTY
and friends
The Pop Princess

Collect all of the Hello Kitty and Friends Stories!

HELLO KITTY
and friends
The Wedding Day

HELLO KITTY
The Beach Holiday

HELLO KITTY
and friends
The Treasure Hunt

HELLO KITTY
and friends
The Talent Show